COUNTING JENNIE

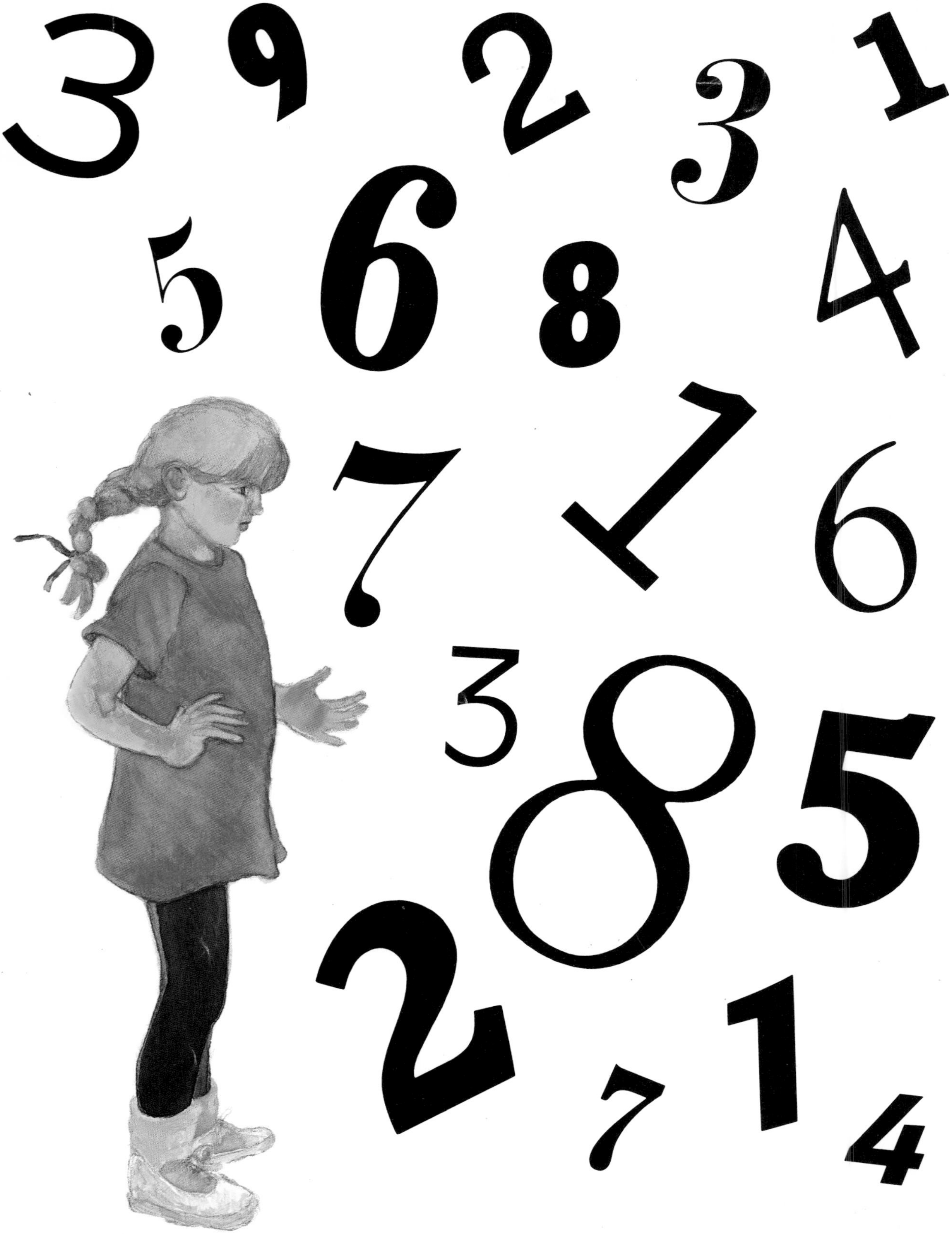
3 9 2 3 1
5 6 8 4
7 1 6
3 8 5
2 7 1 4

COUNTING JENNIE

by Helena Clare Pittman

Carolrhoda Books, Inc./Minneapolis

Manufactured in the
United States of America
1 2 3 4 5 6 P/JR 99 98 97 96 95 94

Library of Congress
Cataloging-in-Publication Data

Pittman, Helena Clare.
  Counting Jennie / by Helena Clare Pittman.
    p.   cm.
  Summary: Jennie counts everything, including
hats, lollipops, and teenagers, on her bus ride to
school.
  ISBN 0-87614-582-9
  [1. Counting—Fiction.] I. Title.
PZ7.P689Co 1994
[E]—dc20   91-41626
                                          CIP
                                          AC

For Jean Hart,
who counts —
with love

Jennie Jinks was a counter. She counted pies and pigeons, cars, crows, and cows. She counted ears of corn, raisins in pudding, meatballs, and french-fried potatoes.

"Three for me, three for Gerald. Three for
Elliot, four for Sarah. Four plus five, or maybe
six," said Jennie. "That leaves ten!"

"Pass the meatballs," said Jennie's brother Elliot.

"*Please* pass the meatballs," said Jennie's father.

"Ten what?" asked Sarah.

"Meatballs for seconds," mumbled Jennie.

"Swallow before you speak, Jennie dear," said Mrs. Jinks.

Jennie counted her sister's
scarves and her mother's shoes.

Her brothers' caps and her
father's ties.

She counted cats and dogs
on the way to the bus stop,
and laundry on clotheslines.

"Thirty-five socks, nine towels, six pairs of pajamas, four pieces of underwear!"

She counted trucks and cars, and when the bus to school was late, bicycles.

"Six with baskets, two with babies."

She counted passengers as they stepped off the bus.

"Three men, two women, and two children."

"Good morning, Jennie," said Nancy the bus driver.

"Good morning," answered Jennie. "One woman, and three more," she whispered on the way to her seat. "Six hats and four ties. Eight men, six children, two teenagers, two skateboards."

"Good morning, Mrs. Riggs,"
said Jennie, taking a seat. "And
one more hat."

Mrs. Riggs smiled. "Good
morning, dear. What did you say?"

"Cherry Street!" called Nancy.

"One bus stop," said Jennie.

A woman wearing a hat and carrying a shopping bag got on.

"Five women, eight hats, one shopping bag," said Jennie.

"Sawyer Square!" shouted Nancy.

"Two bus stops," added Jennie.

Three men got off.

"Minus three equals five."

"Park Circle!" called
Nancy.

"Three," said Jennie.

"Three what?" asked
Mrs. Riggs.

"Bus stops," answered
Jennie politely.

Four men, a woman, and
two children got on.

"Plus four equals nine. One more woman equals six. Two more children make eight. Two teen-agers, two skateboards, two more hats, four more ties!"

"And two balloons," said Mrs. Riggs. "I'd better hurry or I'll miss my stop. Have a good day, Jennie."

"Thank you, Mrs. Riggs. Five women again."

"Zoo!" called Nancy next. "Watch your step!"

"Four," said Jennie.

A woman and two children got off. Two men, three children, a woman and her poodle got on.

"Five women, eleven men, nine children," Jennie counted. "Three pinwheels, six braids, six bows—make that seven—one more balloon, three lollipops...oops!"

One of the children began to cry.

"Two lollipops," said Jennie.

"One dog—make that eight bows."

"Station Street, coming up!" announced Nancy as
the bus sped past the zoo.

"Oh, dear," said Jennie. "Three elephants, three
bears, two lions, a camel!"

"One, two, three, four, five monkeys…"

"Train's waiting!" cried Nancy as the bus turned the corner.

"And five bus stops," said Jennie.

Two men, a woman, and two
children hurried off to catch the train.
" 'Bye, Nancy," called the woman.
" 'Bye, Nancy," said her daughter.
" 'Bye, Nancy," said the girl's sister.

"Minus one leaves four," said
Jennie. "Minus two leaves seven, nine
men, two teenagers, two skateboards."

"Goodness, what's this?"
exclaimed Nancy.

"Parade practice at Market
Street," announced a boy with
a flag.

"One flag, a drum, a triangle, a tuba, two saxophones. Two flutes, three French horns, eleven more teenagers, eleven more hats."

"Scudder next," said Nancy.

"Six," said Jennie.

Two messengers with stacks of deliveries got on at Scudder Street.

"Wow!" Jennie exclaimed. She counted fourteen in one pile. Eleven in the other.

"How's it going, Joe?" inquired one messenger.

"Enough deliveries for a week! How about you, Bob?"

"Same here," agreed Bob.

"Any for Forty-seventh Street?" asked Joe.

"Three," answered Bob.

"Trade you my South Streets for your Forty-sevenths," said Joe.

"Sure!" said Bob.

"Minus three equals eleven," whispered Jennie. "Plus three equals...fourteen again!"

"South and Forty-seventh!" cried Nancy. "Market Street next."

"Seven," said Jennie.

"See ya, Joe," said Bob.

"See ya, Bob," said Joe.

"Nine men again," said Jennie.

"Market Street!" called Nancy. "All passengers for Market Street!"

"Eight," said Jennie. The boy with the flag stood up. So did the other paraders. "Minus a flag, a drum, a triangle, a tuba, two saxophones. Two flutes, three French horns. Minus thirteen teenagers, three children, two women, two men!"

"Leaves seven men, two women, four children, six hats, two ties. No skateboards, no shopping bags, no musical instruments!"

A woman carrying flowers got on, another with plants, and one with a pie. A man got on with fish, another with hats, one with a crate of ducks, another with a crate of geese, and one more with a crate of chickens.

"South and Depot next! Please step to the back of the bus," called Nancy.

"Thirteen tulips, three plants, one pie. Seventeen fish, seventeen ducks, fifteen more hats, twelve geese, fifteen chickens. Three more women, five more men!"

"Bus Depot!"

"Nine," said Jennie.

Another bus pulled up. A crowd of children rushed
off and rushed onto Jennie's bus.

"Please show your tickets!" cried Nancy.
"Ten girls and eight boys," said Jennie.
"School Street next!" shouted Nancy.

At South and School Street, the bus
hit a bump. The door of one of the crates
flew open.

"B-buck-buck-buck!" squawked
chickens, scattering up the aisle.

Geese flapped and honked. Ducks
waddled and quacked. Grown-ups shouted.
Children laughed. Jennie gasped.

"Eleven hens! Four white with gray
speckles, four gray with white speckles, one
brown, one red, one yellow! Four roosters,
one red, one yellow, two white!"

"What a racket!" shouted Nancy.
"There will be a short delay!"

The schoolchildren rushed off the bus.

" 'Bye, Nancy," they called.

" 'Bye, Nancy," called Jennie. "Now
let me see, what does all that come to?"

Suddenly the school bell was clanging. The bus was gone. The school yard was empty.

Jennie ran. She counted forty-three squares in the sidewalk up School Street, fifty-seven bars in the iron fence, fourteen stairs to the front door, and nine bulletin boards from the front door to her classroom.

The door to her classroom was closed. She could hear her teacher's voice. "Christopher, Joshua, and Michael. Katherine, Beverly, Rachel, and Joseph. Twenty-four…"

"Twenty-five!" cried Jennie, opening the door.

Mr. Maxwell looked up.

"Why, Jennie Jinks, you're late. You almost missed arithmetic!"

"Excuse me, Mr. Maxwell," Jennie puffed.

Jennie's teacher smiled. "But we're glad you're here," he said. "That will be twenty-five…counting Jennie."

Here's What Jennie Counted:

33 meatballs
35 socks
9 towels
6 pairs of pajamas
4 pieces of underwear
8 bicycles
8 ties
36 hats
3 balloons
2 skateboards
3 elephants
3 bears
2 lions
1 camel
5 monkeys

15 chickens
17 ducks
12 geese
 1 poodle
 1 flag
 3 French horns
 1 drum
 1 triangle
 1 tuba
 2 saxophones
 2 flutes
17 fish
 1 pie
 3 plants
 1 shopping bag

8 bows
6 braids
25 deliveries
13 tulips
3 pinwheels
3 lollipops
43 sidewalk squares
57 fence bars
14 steps
9 bulletin boards
10 bus stops
12 women
24 men
13 teenagers
31 children . . .
and 1 counter